Mr. Docker Is off His Rocker!

My Weird School #10

Mr. Docker Is Off His Rocker!

Dan Gutman

Pictures by
Jim Paillot

HarperTrophy®
An Imprint of HarperCollinsPublishers

Thanks to "Science Bob" Pflugfelder for some ideas in this book.

Library of Congress Cataloging-in-Publication Data
Gutman, Dan.
 Mr. Docker is off his rocker! / Dan Gutman ; pictures by Jim Paillot.— 1st Harper Trophy ed.
  p. cm. – (My weird school ; #10)
 Summary: Mr. Docker, a new science teacher, is a crazy inventor who blows things up, uses potatoes for power, and has A.J. and his friends wondering whether science is for nerds or is the coolest subject ever.
 ISBN-10: 0-06-082227-9 (pbk.) – ISBN-10: 0-06-082228-7 (lib. bdg.)
 ISBN-13: 978-0-06-082227-9 (pbk.) – ISBN-13: 978-0-06-082228-6 (lib. bdg.)
 [1. Teachers–Fiction. 2. Science–Fiction 3. Schools–Fiction. 4. Humorous stories.]
I. Title: Mister Docker is off his rocker..II. Paillot, Jim, ill. III. Title. IV. Series.
PZ7.G9846Mpu 2006
[Fic]–dc22
                                                                                    2005017971

First Harper Trophy edition, 2006

Visit us on the World Wide Web!
www.harperchildrens.com
16 17 18 19 20 OPM 30 29 28 27

To Emma

Contents

Science
Is for Nerds

My name is A.J. and I hate school.

Why do we need to learn how to read if we have books on CD? Why do we need to learn social studies if that stuff happened a long time ago and we can't do anything about it now? I hate that stuff. But there's one subject I *really* hate.

Andrea Young.

Well, Andrea is not exactly a *subject*. She's this annoying girl in my class. Even her curly brown hair is annoying.

"Guess what, A.J.?" Andrea said as we were putting our backpacks away.

"Your butt," I replied. (Anytime somebody asks, "Guess what?" you should always say, "Your butt." That's the first rule of being a kid.)

"I know what A.J. stands for," Andrea said.

"Do not."

"Do *too*."

We went back and forth like that for a while. There's no way Andrea could know what A.J. stands for. I never told anyone. Even my best friends, Ryan and Michael, don't know. If anyone ever found out what A.J. stands for, I'd have to get a new name. I'd have to leave town.

"A.J. stands for—"

Andrea never got the chance to finish her sentence because our teacher, Miss Daisy, came in.

"Enough chitchatting," Miss Daisy said. "It's time for Show and Share."

Oh man! I forgot all about Show and Share! We were supposed to bring in something that starts with the letter D and tell the class about it. I looked in my desk for a D word. Nothing. I looked in my pockets. All I had was lunch money.

But wait! A dime! "Dime" begins with D!

"I brought in a dime," I told Miss Daisy.

"Good," she said. "What can you tell us about the dime, A.J.?"

"It's worth ten cents," I said, and everybody laughed even though I didn't say anything funny.

Andrea was waving her hand in the air, and she got called on, of course.

"The word 'dime' comes from the Latin word 'decimus,'" Andrea said.

I hate her.

"Very good, Andrea!" said Miss Daisy. "How did you know that?"

"I looked it up in *my* D word," Andrea said. "I brought in a *dictionary*. I use it all the time at home to look up words."

Andrea grinned her little I'm-so-smart grin.

Ryan, who sits next to me, whispered, "If she was *really* smart, she wouldn't *have* to look stuff up."

"Andrea, would you please look up the word 'science'?" asked Miss Daisy. "S-C-I-E-N-C-E."

What a dumb spelling! There's no reason why that word should have a C in it. Andrea turned the pages of her dictionary.

"S . . . S-A . . . S-C," she said. "Here it is. 'Science is knowledge made up of an orderly system of facts that have been learned from study, observation, and experiments.'"

"Very good!"

Andrea smiled her I-know-everything smile and said she was going to keep her dictionary on her desk from now on in case she had to look up any other words.

Why can't a box of dictionaries fall on her head?

"I have good news," Miss Daisy said. "We have a new teacher at Ella Mentry School. His name is Mr. Docker, and he used to be a real scientist. He's retired now, but he agreed to come back to school to teach us science."

That was good news? It sounded like bad news to me. We never had to learn science before. Now, just because some old guy doesn't like being retired, we had to learn a new subject. It wasn't fair.

Why did I have to learn science? It's not like I was going to be a scientist someday. When I grow up, I'm going to be a football player. I play Pee Wee football. Tackling people is fun.

Suddenly Mr. Klutz, our principal, poked his bald head into the doorway.

"Has anybody seen Mr. Docker?" he asked. "I think he ran away."

"We'd better line up in ABC order and go look for him!" said Miss Daisy. "Quickly! To the science room!"

I didn't need any dictionary to tell me what science is. Science is for nerds.

The Power of the Potato

We walked a million hundred miles to the science room. Michael, who never ties his shoes, was the line leader.

"Science is for nerds," I said.

"Science is fun!" said Andrea, who thinks everything about school is fun.

The science room is probably the

weirdest room in the history of the world. In the corner there was a skeleton wearing a top hat. There was a cage with white mice running around it. There were strange machines, microscopes, computers, plants, and other stuff all over the place.

"This place is freaky weird," Ryan said.

"Where's Mr. Docker?" Andrea asked.

"I don't know," said Miss Daisy, who doesn't know anything.

We were looking at all the junk when the door banged open and an old guy came in. He was standing on one of those rolling things that looks like an old-time lawn mower. He was wearing a helmet, goggles, and one of those doctor lab coats. What a nerd!

"Hi, everybody!" he said. "I'm Mr. Docker!" Then he smashed into the chalkboard and fell off his rolling thing. We all

ran over to pick him up off the floor.

"Are you okay?" we all asked.

"Never better!"

Mr. Docker took off his helmet and goggles. He had crazy gray hair that went off in all directions. It looked like he hadn't combed it in years. If my hair looked like that, my mother wouldn't let me out of the house.

"Hey, I've seen that guy before," Ryan whispered. "He lives down the street from me!"

Mr. Docker reached into his lab coat and pulled out a potato. He took a bite out of it.

"Sorry I'm late," Mr. Docker said. "I had

to harvest my tubers."

Huh? I didn't know what he was talking about.

"Tubers are potatoes," Andrea said. "I looked it up in the dictionary once."

"Very good," Mr. Docker said. "Welcome to science. I'm going to take you on a scientific journey. We're going to explore the wonders of our world. The future is in your hands. You will be the scientists of tomorrow."

"Not me," I said. "I'm going to be a football player."

"But we can *all* be scientists," Mr. Docker said. "All you have to do is look around and ask 'Why?' Why does the

Earth spin? Why do dogs wag their tails? Can anybody think of another science why question?"

"Why do we have to learn science?" I asked.

Andrea looked at me and rolled her eyes.

"That's a good question," Mr. Docker said.

I stuck out my tongue at Andrea. Nah-nah-nah boo-boo on her!

"We have to learn science because science is all around us," Mr. Docker said. "When you bounce a ball, you're learning the science of physics. When you look at a flower, you're learning the science of botany. When you pick your nose, you're learning the science of biology."

"You're also getting the boogers out," I added.

Ryan said he was a scientist because he went on the Internet and found out how to make a stink bomb.

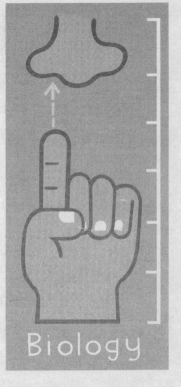

Biology

"We're all scientists," Mr. Docker said, "and kids make great scientists, because you're naturally curious. I love it when kids ask why questions. Does anyone have another why question?"

"Why can't we go to recess?" I asked.

"Science is more fun than recess," Mr. Docker said as he took something out of his desk drawer. "Hey, let me show you something. I brought this from my laboratory at home."

"What is it?" asked Emily.

"It's a potato clock," Mr. Docker said. "There are no batteries. You don't plug it into an outlet on the wall. It's powered by the chemicals in potatoes! Watch this!"

He took two potatoes out of his desk and put them in the clock. Then he took the wires that went from the clock and stuck them into the potatoes. The little

screen on the clock lit up and said "10:15."

"It works!" we all shouted. "Wow! That's cool!"

"I love potatoes!" said Mr. Docker. Then he let out this cackling laugh, just like scientists do in the movies. That's a sure sign that somebody is crazy.

"Why did you make a clock out of potatoes?" Andrea asked.

"I wanted to see time fry!" said Mr. Docker. "Get it? Time fry? Potatoes? French fries?"

I laughed at his joke, even though it wasn't very funny. My friend Billy who lives around the corner told me that if a teacher makes a joke and you don't laugh, they get mad and give you extra homework. So always laugh at your teacher's jokes, no matter how bad they are. That's the first rule of being a kid.

"But seriously," Mr. Docker said, "the Earth is going to run out of oil someday.

We'll need to use other forms of energy."

"Like potato power?" I asked.

"Exactly!" Mr. Docker said. "Imagine, if two potatoes can make enough energy to run a clock, what could two *hundred* potatoes run? Or two *thousand*? Or two *million*?"

Mr. Docker is a real potato freak. But as he was talking, his potato clock stopped.

"What time is it?" Michael asked.

"Time to change potatoes," said Mr. Docker. Then he let out his evil, demented, cackling laugh again.

Mr. Docker is off his rocker!

Stop, Drop, and Roll

Andrea was so obnoxious with her dictionary. Every five minutes she looked up another word so she could show how smart she is.

But I got her. When she went to the bathroom during cleanup time, I snuck over to her desk and opened the dictionary. I flipped through the pages until I found the word "stupid." Then I drew a picture of Andrea and a line pointing to the word.

It was great. You should have been there. I closed the dictionary just before Andrea came back from the bathroom. Nah-nah-nah boo-boo on her! I couldn't wait for her to find the picture.

Miss Daisy told us to line up for science. We walked a million hundred miles to the science room. Mr. Docker wasn't there yet, but then he rolled in on that lawn mower thing. He was eating potato chips. Mr. Docker sure loves potatoes.

"Sorry I'm late," he said. "I was reading

a book about helium, and I just couldn't put it down." And then he did that cackling demented laugh, so we had to laugh so he wouldn't give us extra homework.

Mr. Docker told us that he is eighty years old and he has seen a lot of science in his life. When he was a kid, they didn't have important stuff like microwave popcorn or Velcro or sneakers that light up when you walk.

"Wow!" I said. "Do you remember when they discovered fire? Were you there when they invented the wheel?"

"I'm not quite that old," Mr. Docker said. "But when I was your age, they didn't have video games."

"No video games?" I asked. "How did you survive?"

"I did experiments!" he said. "Let's do an experiment right now. What do you think would happen if we combined water with the chemicals citric acid and sodium bicarbonate?"

"Beats me," Michael said.

"Let's do the experiment to find out!" said Mr. Docker.

He took one of those tiny little plastic cans they use to hold camera film and put hot water in it. He dropped in a piece of Alka-Seltzer, which is this medicine my dad takes when he has a tummy ache. Then he snapped the top on the film can and put it upside down on the floor.

Nothing happened for a few seconds. Then the film can suddenly shot up into the air and bounced off the ceiling.

"The chemical reaction gives off carbon dioxide gas," said Mr. Docker. "The can has nowhere to go, so it blasts off!"

Wow! Even I had to admit that was cool.

Mr. Docker told us that scientists use something called the scientific method.

"First think of a question or problem," he said. "Then try to guess what the answer is. After that do an experiment. Then look at the results and form a conclusion. That's the scientific method."

Mr. Docker asked if anyone had any questions, and Andrea (of course) stuck her hand in the air.

"I have a why question," Andrea said. "Why is the sky blue?"

What a brownnoser. Everybody knows why the sky is blue. It's because air is blue.

"The sky is blue because of Roy G. Biv," Mr. Docker said.

"Roy G. Biv?" I said. "Who's that?"

"He's right outside," Mr. Docker said.

He took out this glass thing that was shaped like a triangle. He brought it over to the window where the sun was shining in.

"This is called a prism," he told us. "It's going to help us find Roy G. Biv."

Mr. Docker held the prism thing up to the sunlight, and the most amazing thing in the history of the world happened. A big old rainbow appeared on the wall of the room. It was cool.

"Roy G. Biv stands for red, orange, yellow, green, blue, indigo, and violet," said Mr. Docker. "Sunlight is made of these different colors. The prism separates them. But when sunlight goes through air, the light particles scatter and bounce off the oxygen atoms. Most of the colors don't scatter very well. But blue scatters really well in all different directions. It has a short wavelength. That's why the sky looks blue."

Andrea was taking notes the whole time. What is her problem?

"See?" Mr. Docker said. "Just about anything is science."

"I know something that's not science," I said. "Blowing stuff up. Blowing stuff up is cool."

"Blowing things up is dangerous," Andrea said.

"Can you possibly be any more boring?" I asked.

"You're both right," said Mr. Docker. "Blowing stuff up is cool *and* dangerous. It's science, too. We can't blow stuff up here, but that gives me a good idea for a what-if experiment. What do you think will happen if I take some raw sodium and put it into water?"

"It will get wet," I said.

"It will melt," said Andrea.

"I think it will float," guessed Ryan.

"Those are good guesses," said Mr. Docker. "Let's do the experiment and find out! Then we'll look at the results and form a conclusion."

Mr. Docker poured water into a pan. He put on a pair of goggles. Then he unlocked a cabinet and took out a chunk of sodium with a big spoon.

"Don't try this at home, kids," he said.

He dropped the chunk of sodium into the pan. And then the most amazing thing in the history of the world happened.

There was a big flash of light! It lit up the whole room! A flame jumped out of the pan! It was way cool, and we saw it live and in person.

"The chemical reaction creates heat!" said Mr. Docker.

Just then something crazy happened. His hair caught on fire!

"Uh-oh," said Mr. Docker. "That's not supposed to happen."

Flames and smoke were coming off his head! It was like his head was a campfire! It was a real Kodak moment.

"Stick your head in the sink!" Michael yelled.

"Stop, drop, and roll!" said Andrea.

"Throw dirt on him!" somebody else yelled.

But we couldn't do any of those things. Mr. Docker went running out of the room, screaming that his head was on fire. He ran pretty fast for an old guy. It was cool.

Maybe science isn't so nerdy after all.

Going on a Field Trip

I learned an important lesson in science class. If you mix raw sodium with water, your head will catch on fire.

Mr. Docker wasn't in school for a few days after "the incident." We were worried about him.

But finally, the day before spring

vacation, Mr. Docker was back at school and we had science class. I almost didn't recognize him. He had a lot less hair. He looked more normal. Mr. Docker should have set his head on fire a long time ago, if you ask me.

"Mr. Docker, where do bugs go in the winter?" Michael asked.

"Some of them dig holes in the ground," said Mr. Docker. "Some go to sleep. Some die."

"That's so sad!" said Emily. What a cry-baby!

"Can we pick our noses and look at the boogers under the microscope?" I asked.

"Not today," said Mr. Docker. "Today

we're going on a field trip."

"Hooray!" everybody shouted. Field trips are cool because we get to leave school. Any place that isn't school is better than school.

"Where are we going on our field trip?" asked Andrea.

"To a field, of course!" said Mr. Docker.

"That's why it's called a field trip."

"Booooo!" I said. "Fields are boring. We should go someplace cool, like a skate park."

We had to walk a million hundred miles to the field behind the school. Then we had to walk around some more in the field.

To Mr. Docker, everything is science. Every five seconds he would stop and tell us the name of some tree. He picked up leaves and showed them to us. He threw a rock into the pond and told us about the ripples in the water. We watched the birds and smelled the flowers.

The best part was when Mr. Docker let

us take a rest and have some pretzels he brought along. We all sat down on a big log. To Mr. Docker, even a dumb log is science.

"Part of this wood is rotted away," he said. "Let's see what's inside."

He pulled off a piece of the log and we saw the most amazing thing in the history of the world—bugs were crawling all over.

"Eeeeek!" shouted the girls. They got off the log and started screaming their heads off.

"Kill them!" shouted the boys. We grabbed sticks and started hitting the log.

"Don't be afraid," Mr. Docker said. "Bugs are our friends."

"Oh yeah?" said Ryan. "Well, one of our friends is on Emily."

It was true. This big, black, disgusting thing was crawling up Emily's arm.

"Eeeeek!" she screamed, and then she went running around in circles. It was hilarious. What a crybaby!

Mr. Docker got down on his hands and knees and started telling us about the little critters on the log. Nobody wanted to touch them.

"Relax," Mr. Docker said, and he actually picked up some gross bug with his fingers. "It's just a beetle grub."

And then he did the most amazing thing in the history of the world. Mr.

Docker took that beetle grub and put it in his *mouth*!

"Ewwwwwwwwwwwwwwwwww!"

We thought we were gonna die. Even Ryan was grossed out, and he'll eat just about anything.

"Mmmm," Mr. Docker said as he chewed the bug. "This makes a better snack than pretzels. Try it. You just have to squeeze the larva to clean its intestines out."

"Ewwwwwwwwwwwwwwwwww!"

"Bugs are good for you," Mr. Docker told us. "They have more protein than steak. People all over the world eat bugs. Did you know that if you lick a slug,

your tongue gets numb?"

"I think I'm gonna throw up," I said.

"What's the big deal?" asked Mr. Docker. "People eat cows, pigs, shrimp, lobster. Bugs are animals too. They can be fried, roasted, or made into soup. Sometimes I sprinkle them on my cereal."

"Ewwwwwwwwwwwwwwwwww!"

I had to admit that the *idea* of eating bugs was cool, but that didn't mean I was going to eat one. All in all, we were totally grossed out.

When we got back to school, Mr. Docker told us he had exciting news.

"We're going to put on a science fair!" he said. "I want everybody to think of a what-if question and design an experiment to answer it. Bring your experiment in on Monday after vacation."

What? We had to spend our vacation

doing work? That's totally not fair!

"I'm going to go home and think of a good what-if question tonight," Andrea said, "so I'll have the whole vacation to work on my experiment."

That gave me an idea for a what-if question. What if a tree full of bugs fell on Andrea's head?

The Science (Not) Fair

Vacations are the best. No school for a whole week! No teachers yelling at you to stop talking. No homework. No getting up early. No Andrea.

My family went to the beach. I didn't think about school once. It was great.

But then came Monday, the worst day

of the week. When I got on the bus for school, I was tired because I had to get up so early.

"Good morning," I grunted to Mrs. Kormel, the bus driver.

"Bingle boo," Mrs. Kormel replied. Mrs. Kormel is not normal.

I thought I was in some weird science fiction movie. All the kids on the bus had strange stuff on their laps. One kid had two soda bottles stuck together, and he

was shaking them to make a little tornado. One kid had a microscope. One kid had a bunch of balloons.

Then I remembered—the science fair!

I sat next to Ryan. He had some boxes of cereal and a big magnet. He said he was going to find out how much iron was in each kind of cereal.

All morning I tried to think of an excuse for not bringing in an experiment. I couldn't say my dog ate it because I used that one last time. Besides, I don't have a dog.

Finally it was time for science. Mr. Docker came to our class so we wouldn't have to carry our experiments to the science room. Everybody had an experiment on their desk.

Everybody but me.

"Didn't you do an experiment, A.J.?" asked Andrea. "You're going to be in trouble."

"So is your face," I said.

Let me give you some advice. If you ever get stuck and you don't know what to say to somebody, just say, "So is your face." If somebody says you're ugly or some other mean thing, just say, "So is your face." There's nothing they can say. You really can't go wrong with "So is your face."

Everybody started asking Mr. Docker questions.

"How can you tell the difference between a crocodile and an alligator?" Emily asked.

"Alligators have bigger snouts," said Mr. Docker.

Wow, Mr. Docker knows everything!

"Is a zebra white with black stripes or black with white stripes?" Michael asked.

"You'll have to shave a zebra to find out," said Mr. Docker. "But we don't have time for questions today. I'm anxious to see your experiments. Let's start with the A people."

Why do we always have to do stuff in ABC order? I always have to go first!

Luckily, Miss I-know-everything had

her hand up, so she got to go first. Andrea brought a big cardboard box up to the front of the room.

"My what-if question was, What if I played music to flowers?" Andrea said. "What kind would help them grow?"

That had to be the dumbest experiment in the history of the world.

Inside the box Andrea had four flower-pots. She made all these charts and graphs to show what she did. Teachers love that stuff.

"I played Beethoven for flower number one," Andrea said. "Flower number two heard jazz music. Flower number three listened to rock and roll. And with flower number four, I sang the songs of my favorite show, *Annie*."

Andrea started singing that dumb song about the sun coming out tomorrow.

"I'm surprised that flower number four didn't die," I whispered to Ryan.

"And what was your conclusion, Andrea?" asked Mr. Docker.

"Number four grew tallest," she said. "So my conclusion is that flowers like to hear me sing."

That's more than I can say for human beings.

"You get an A," said Mr. Docker. "Who's next? A.J.?"

"A.J. didn't do an experiment," Andrea

said as she was putting her box away.

"I did too," I said.

"It must be invisible."

"So is your face," I said.

I walked up to the front of the room. I didn't know what to do. I didn't know what to say. I had to think fast.

"My what-if question was, What if you don't feed a fish?" I said.

"I beg your pardon?" asked Mr. Docker.

"My chore at home is to put food in our fish tank," I said. "Well, we went on vacation to the beach last week. So as an *experiment*, I didn't put food in the fish tank."

"Um-hmm," said Mr. Docker.

"Then we came home and I looked at the result," I said.

"And what was the result?" asked Mr. Docker.

"The fish was dead."

"No food, eh?" said Mr. Docker.

"Well, I gave it plenty of water," I said.

"And your conclusion?"

"Without food, living things die," I said.

"Awesome experiment!" Ryan whispered when I got back to my seat. "You should get the Nobel Prize."

Andrea stood up, like she was all mad.

"That was no experiment!" she said. "You just forgot to feed your fish and you *killed* it! You're such a dumbhead!"

"Oh, you sing to flowers and you call *me* a dumbhead?" I said right back. "Flowers don't even have ears!"

Mr. Docker told me and Andrea to calm down.

"I feel bad about your fish, A.J.," he said. "But I must admit, you used the scientific method. So I'm giving you an A."

I stuck my tongue out at Andrea. Ha-ha!

In her face! She spent the whole vacation working on a dumb experiment while I was having fun boogie boarding! And I still got an A! Nah-nah-nah boo-boo on her! It was the greatest moment of my life.

"What kind of fish was it?" Mr. Docker asked me.

"A sucker barb," I said, and everyone laughed just because "sucker" is a funny word.

"Can you tell us anything about sucker barbs, A.J.?"

I didn't know a thing about sucker barbs. I never even paid any attention to our fish. That's probably why I forgot to feed it before we went on vacation.

"I'll look sucker barbs up in my dictionary," said Andrea. She started flipping through the pages. "S . . . S-H . . . S-P . . . S-T—"

Suddenly Andrea stopped and screamed.

"What's the matter, Andrea?" asked Mr. Docker.

"Somebody drew a mean picture in my dictionary!"

Being Nice to Andrea

"It was *you*!" Andrea yelled. "You drew the picture of me in my dictionary next to the word 'stupid'!"

It was recess. She had dragged me to the big turtle so nobody could hear what she was saying.

"I did not," I lied.

"Did too."

We went back and forth like that for a while.

"You'd better be nice to me," Andrea said, "or I'm going to tell everyone what A.J. stands for."

"You don't even know what A.J. stands for," I said. "You're just trying to get me to tell. I know your tricks."

Andrea said her mother is vice president of the PTA (Parents who Talk Alot), and she can find out anything about anybody. Then she whispered in my ear.

"A.J. stands for . . ."

And then she said it.

Oh no! She was *right*!

She knew! I thought I was gonna die. Andrea was gonna tell everyone. They'd be making fun of me forever. I'd never hear the end of it. My life was over!

I had no choice. There was only one thing I could do.

I would have to be nice to Andrea.

When recess was over, Miss Daisy asked us to pick a partner and work on our social studies worksheet.

"Hey A.J.," Andrea said, loud enough for everyone to hear, "do you want to be my study buddy?"

Most of the time I work with Ryan or Michael. I would rather die than be study buddies with Andrea. But I would also rather die than have everyone know what A.J. stands for.

"Okay," I said.

I was nice to Andrea all afternoon. It was the worst afternoon of my life. Finally three o'clock came. Time to go home. Miss Daisy told us to clean up. Just before the bell rang, Andrea dropped her pencil box on the floor. Pencils rolled all over.

"A.J.," Andrea said, "be a

dear and pick up my pencils."

Any other day I would laugh at her and tell her to pick up her own dumb pencils. But this wasn't any other day. This was the day I found out that Andrea knew what A.J. stands for.

I picked up her dumb pencils.

On the bus home, I wanted to sit alone, but Ryan and Michael grabbed seats next to me.

"You sure were nice to Andrea today," Ryan said.

"I saw her talking to you near the big turtle," said Michael.

"Oooooh!" Ryan said. "A.J. and Andrea are in *love*!"

"When are you gonna get married?" asked Michael.

If those guys weren't my best friends, I would hate them.

The Truth About Mr. Docker

"Mr. Docker, if I weigh sixty pounds," Michael asked when we got to the science room, "how much would I weigh on the moon?"

"About ten pounds," said Mr. Docker, who knows everything.

"My mother should go to the moon," I

said. "She's always trying to lose weight."

"Mr. Docker, when I smell something really bad," asked Ryan, "is that yucky thing inside my nose?"

"Well, yes, tiny particles of it," said Mr. Docker. "The air carries dust, chemicals, and even animals! Some of that clings to the hairs of your nose."

"Gross!"

Just having *hair* in your nose is disgusting! Not to mention all that other stuff.

"No more questions today," Mr. Docker said. "I want to show you something."

He had a big pot on his desk, and smoke was coming out of it.

"What's that?" Andrea asked.

"Liquid nitrogen," said Mr. Docker. "It's a gas that has been turned into a very cold liquid. Now don't try this at home, kids."

He took a long rose and dipped it in the pot. Then he took it out and hit the rose against the chalkboard. The rose petals cracked off like they were potato chips!

"Cool!" we all said.

"It's so cool, it's three hundred fifty degrees below zero," Mr. Docker said.

Then he blew up a balloon and dipped it in the liquid nitrogen. When he took it out, it was tiny.

"Cold air makes things smaller," said

Mr. Docker. "Now watch this."

He took a piece of wood out of his desk drawer. There was a nail sticking out of it. Then he took a banana and held it in the liquid nitrogen for about a minute. When he took it out, he started whacking the nail into the piece of wood with the banana! Cool! I never saw anybody hammer in a nail with a banana before.

After science we went to the vomitorium for lunch. Usually I shoot straw wrappers at Andrea and her annoying friends at the next table. But I had to be nice to her because I didn't want her telling everybody what A.J. stands for.

Andrea and Emily came over to our table.

"Is anyone sitting here?" Andrea asked.

Usually I would say something obnoxious like "The Invisible Man is sitting here, so get lost." But I didn't.

"You can sit there," I said. Michael and Ryan giggled and made kissy faces.

Ryan gave me his cupcake and I gave him my asparagus. Ryan will eat anything.

"I wonder what Mr. Docker is eating," Michael said. "Probably spiders."

"Yeah," Ryan said, "I bet he's sprinkling them on his cereal."

"That's crazy," I said. "Nobody eats cereal for lunch."

"Something tells me that if you sprinkle bugs on your food," said Andrea, "you don't care which meal it is."

"Mr. Docker sure is weird," Emily said.

"Maybe he's not a science teacher at all," I said. "Did you ever think of that?"

"What do you mean?" asked Emily.

"Maybe he's just pretending to be a science teacher," I said.

"Yeah," said Ryan. "Maybe he's a mad

scientist who kidnaps real science teachers and swaps brains with them. Stuff like that happens all the time, you know."

"It does?"

"Stop trying to scare Emily," said Andrea.

"Think about it," Michael said. "Mr. Docker told us he has a laboratory at home. He wears a lab coat. He has a weird laugh. He eats bugs. And he uses a banana for a hammer. He's *got* to be a mad scientist!"

"Maybe Mr. Docker is a loony who brainwashes people," Ryan suggested.

"Brainwash?" Emily was shaking. "What's that?"

"That's a shampoo for bald guys," I said. "They don't have any hair, so they wash their brains."

"No it's not," Ryan said. "I saw brain-washing in a movie. They hook wires up to your head and wipe out your memory so you don't remember anything. Then they program you to turn evil."

"We've got to do something!" said Emily, and she went running out of the vomitorium. Emily is weird.

"She's right, you know," Andrea said. "We can't let Mr. Docker get away with brainwashing our real science teacher."

"What can we do?" asked Michael.

"Mr. Docker lives down the street from

me," Ryan said. "We can spy on him."

"Then we can thwart his evil plan," I said. I always wanted to say "thwart." It's a cool word. I saw it in a comic book once.

We agreed to go on a secret spying mission at Mr. Docker's house on Saturday.

Shh! Don't tell anybody!

Don't Try This at Home

It was Friday, the day before our big spy mission. Mr. Docker had a bunch of cardboard milk cartons on his desk, and some little square mirrors, too.

"What are we going to do with this stuff?" I asked.

"We're going to make periscopes!" he said.

"I saw a submarine movie where they used a periscope to see above the water," said Ryan.

"In Greek, 'peri' means 'around,'" said Mr. Docker, "and 'scopus' means 'to look.'"

Mr. Docker helped us cut holes in our milk cartons and glue the mirrors inside so we could see around corners. It was cool, and we each got to take our periscope home.

"Mr. Docker, does outer space ever end?" asked Andrea.

"That's one of the great mysteries of the universe," Mr. Docker said. "I don't know if we'll ever know the answer."

"Why do birds fly, Mr. Docker?" Ryan asked.

"It's faster than driving," said Mr. Docker, and everybody laughed even though it wasn't very funny.

Lately, I'd noticed, Mr. Docker wasn't giving us very good answers. It was like he was getting sick of hearing our why questions.

Miss Lazar, the custodian, came into the science room with a big ladder.

"Hooray for Miss Lazar!" everyone chanted.

Mr. Docker handed Miss Lazar a bowling ball with a rope attached to it. She went up the ladder and tied the rope to the ceiling, so the bowling ball hung down.

"Duty calls," said Miss Lazar, and she left. We all laughed, because Miss Lazar said "duty" and it sounds just like "doody."

"This is a pendulum," said Mr. Docker.

He took the bowling ball and walked backward, pulling the bowling ball with him. Then he put the ball against his nose.

"What do you think will happen if I let go of this pendulum?" he asked.

"It will swing across the room and come back and smash you in the head," Ryan said.

"Let's do the experiment and find out," said Mr. Docker.

"No! Don't!" we all shouted, but Mr. Docker let go of the ball anyway.

"Eeeeeeek!" all the girls shouted as the bowling ball swung across the room.

"Get out of the way!" shouted Michael.

Mr. Docker just stood there!

"We've got to do something!" shouted Emily.

She was right. The bowling ball was heading back to Mr. Docker, straight for his head! I had to act fast!

I remembered my Pee Wee football training. At the last possible second, I jumped up and tackled Mr. Docker. He fell backward. We crashed into the skeleton in the corner. Bones went flying everywhere and the skeleton was destroyed, but I had saved Mr. Docker's life. All those football practices paid off!

"Why did you do that, A.J.?" Mr. Docker asked as we were lying on the floor.

"I didn't want the bowling ball to hit you in the face," I said.

"It wasn't going to hit me," Mr. Docker said. "A swinging pendulum loses energy because of gravity and air resistance. That's what I was trying to show."

"Oh," I said. "Sorry."

Maybe he was right, but if you ask me, a grown man shouldn't stand in front of a moving bowling ball.

Spying on Mr. Docker

Spying on people is cool. My sister, Amy, and I spy on our parents all the time. We tiptoe around and hide behind the furniture so we can write down their conversations. I always hope to hear good secrets, but all my parents ever talk about is whose turn it is to take out the garbage and stuff like that. They're the most boring parents in the history of the world.

On Saturday me, Michael, Andrea, and Emily rode our bikes to Ryan's house. Ryan was all ready. He had sunglasses for all of us, because spies always wear sunglasses. He had his milk carton

periscope. Ryan even had one of his famous stink bombs.

"Okay," he said, "let's synchronize our potato clock."

"What does that mean?" Emily asked.

"I don't know," Ryan said. "But they always synchronize their watches in spy movies."

We tiptoed down the street to Mr. Docker's house. It looked pretty normal. You would never know a mad scientist lived there.

We hid behind a tree across the street. Ryan looked in the periscope.

"Can you see anything?" Andrea asked.

"No."

"Maybe he's not home," said Emily. "We should go."

"Let's get closer," I said.

We tiptoed across the street and sneaked up Mr. Docker's driveway.

"If he comes home right now, we'll be in big trouble," Emily said.

"Don't be a baby," I said. "Come on. Let's peek in the window."

I looked in the window. I was hoping to see Mr. Docker swapping brains with someone, but there was nobody inside.

"He's not home," Andrea said. "Let's get out of here."

"Oops."

I turned around. Ryan dropped the

stink bomb in the middle of Mr. Docker's driveway! It broke open and the stink got out.

"Ewww, it's disgusting!" Andrea said, holding her nose.

"Ugh, I think I'm gonna die," I said.

I didn't think things could get any

worse, but they did. Suddenly the garage door opened!

Mr. Docker was standing there!

He had a knife in his hand!

We all screamed!

"He's crazy!" Andrea shouted. "Run for your life!"

The Spudmobile

That crazy mad scientist Mr. Docker was four feet away, and he was holding a big, sharp knife. I looked at Ryan. Ryan looked at Michael. Michael looked at me. Andrea and Emily ran away.

"Are you going to swap our b-b-brains?" I asked Mr. Docker.

"What are you d-d-doing with that knife?" asked Ryan.

"I'm peeling potatoes," Mr. Docker said. "What's that smell?"

"I made a stink bomb," Ryan said.

"Excellent!" said Mr. Docker. "I'm glad you're doing science projects at home.

Welcome to my laboratory."

We looked around Mr. Docker's garage. It was filled with lots of test tubes, jars of chemicals, and other stuff. But the thing that stood out was his car. It didn't have a metal covering like a normal car. The whole thing was covered with . . . potatoes!

"What's *that*?" Michael asked.

"You're just in time," Mr. Docker said. "I've been working on it for months and it's finally done. Behold the Spudmobile!"

The car was covered with rows and rows of potatoes. Each potato had wires attached to it that went to the engine. It was the weirdest-looking car I ever saw.

"You built a car powered by potatoes?" Ryan asked.

"It can also run on pickles," Mr. Docker replied. "But I thought a Picklemobile would sound silly. Do you want a ride?"

"Sure!" we said as we climbed in.

"It has that new potato car smell," said Michael.

"What kind of mileage does this thing get?" asked Ryan, who knows a lot about cars.

"About five miles per potato," said Mr. Docker.

He turned the key. The engine started up with a quiet hum. Mr. Docker pulled out of the driveway. It really worked!

"Maybe someday *all* cars will run on potatoes," Mr. Docker said. "They won't have gas stations anymore. They'll have potato stations."

"And if you're out driving and you get hungry," I said, "you can eat your car."

"The possibilities are endless!" said Mr. Docker. "We could heat our houses with potatoes! Someday we'll have potato-powered computers and TV sets."

"They could have potato-powered toys," I suggested. "Potatoes not included."

Mr. Docker let out one of his cackling laughs. That's when I realized that he's not an evil mad scientist at all. Mr. Docker is the coolest nerd in the history of the world!

We turned the corner, and there were Andrea and Emily on the sidewalk.

They were staring at the potato car with their mouths wide open, like they were looking at a ghost.

"Check it out!" Ryan shouted out the window. "We're riding in the Spudmobile!"

"Power to the potato!" shouted Michael.

"Nah-nah-nah boo-boo on you!" I shouted.

My Buzzing, Bubbling Brain

I could hardly sleep that night. My brain wouldn't stop thinking about Mr. Docker and his amazing potato car. Lots of why questions were buzzing around in my head. I decided that science isn't nerdy after all. Science is cool! I don't want to be a football player anymore. When I grow

up, I want to be a scientist like Mr. Docker.

By the time I got to school, my brain was bubbling over with why questions.

"Miss Daisy," I asked as soon as she

walked in the class, "why do some people have curly hair and other people have straight hair? Why is grass green? Why is it called a pair of pants when you only have one of them?"

"I have no idea," said Miss Daisy, who doesn't know anything. "I'm surprised to hear you asking all these questions, A.J. Didn't you say science was for nerds?"

"Cool nerds," I said.

"We have science this morning," she said. "Maybe Mr. Docker can answer your questions."

I couldn't wait to get to the science room. Mr. Docker was in there, eating potato salad.

"Mr. Docker," I asked. "Why don't eggs break under a chicken? How come heavy boats can float but light rocks sink? Do cats have belly buttons?"

"Whoa!" said Mr. Docker. "Slow down, A.J.!"

"Why does my dad have hair growing out of his ears?" I asked. "How do microwave ovens work? What would happen if I dropped a watermelon off the Empire State Building?"

"A.J., I think I'm getting a headache," said Mr. Docker.

"Where do babies come from, Mr. Docker? Is a tomato a fruit or a vegetable? Why is water wet? How many toothpicks can you make out of one tree?"

"That's enough, A.J.!" said Mr. Docker.

"Why do clocks go clockwise, Mr. Docker?" I asked. "Why do leaves change color? Why is ice slippery? If you don't milk a cow, will the cow explode?"

"Stop, A.J.!" shouted Mr. Docker.

"Why are bubbles round, Mr. Docker? Why do we sneeze? What's the difference between jelly and jam? How come when cartoon characters run off cliffs, they don't fall right away? Why do grown-ups like vegetables? How come some people can roll their tongues and other people can't? Where did Mr. Klutz's hair go? Why does the moon look bigger than the sun?"

"I can't take it anymore!" Mr. Docker shouted.

Then he ran out of the room. His head wasn't even on fire, but it was cool anyway.

The Worst Moment of My Life

We had to let Andrea sit with us in the vomitorium because I was still being nice to her. My mom packed me a jelly sandwich because it was meat loaf day and I hate meat loaf.

"I love meat loaf," said Andrea. "It goes so well with mashed potatoes."

What a waste, I thought, looking at Andrea's mashed potatoes. Those potatoes could be powering someone's car or washing machine.

Suddenly Mr. Klutz came running into the vomitorium.

"Has anybody seen Mr. Docker?" asked Mr. Klutz. "He ran away again."

Everybody looked at me.

"A.J. drove him crazy," said Andrea, the big tattletale. "He asked Mr. Docker so many why questions that he went running out of the room."

"It's not my fault!" I said. "Mr. Docker was crazy long before I got to him."

"It is too your fault!"

"Is not!"

We went back and forth like that for a while. Finally I got sick of listening to Andrea. I scooped up some of her mashed potatoes and mashed them right on top of her head! Ha-ha-ha!

"Eeeeeek!" Andrea screamed. "I'm covered in potatoes!"

"So is your face!" I yelled.

Andrea got up and stood on her chair.

"Hey everybody!" she yelled. "I have an announcement. I know what A.J. stands for. A.J. stands for . . . Arlo Jervis!"

No!

She said it! I couldn't believe she actually said it! Out loud!

I didn't know what to say. I didn't know what to do. I had to think fast.

So I did the only thing I could do. I ran out of the vomitorium. I ran out of the school. I ran home.

And that's where I'm going to stay for the rest of my life.

Maybe after a million hundred years go

by, everybody will forget that A.J. stands for Arlo Jervis. Maybe then I'll be able to go back to school and face my friends again. Maybe then I'll be able to return to a normal life.

But it won't be easy!

Check out the My Weird School series!

Pb 0-06-050700-4   Pb 0-06-050704-7   Pb 0-06-074518-5

Pb 0-06-050702-0   Pb 0-06-050706-3

#1: Miss Daisy Is Crazy!

The first book in the hilarious series stars A.J., a second grader who hates school—and can't believe his teacher hates it too!

#2: Mr. Klutz Is Nuts!

A.J. can't believe his crazy principal wants to climb to the top of the flagpole!

#3: Mrs. Roopy Is Loopy!

The new librarian at A.J.'s weird school thinks she's George Washington one day and Little Bo Peep the next!

#4: Ms. Hannah Is Bananas!

Ms. Hannah, the art teacher, wears clothes made from pot holders and collects trash. Worse than that, she's trying to make A.J. be partners with yucky Andrea!

#5: Miss Small Is off the Wall!

Miss Small, the gym teacher, is teaching A.J.'s class to juggle scarves, balance feathers, and do everything *but* play sports!

HarperTrophy®
An Imprint of HarperCollinsPublishers

Pb 0-06-074520-7   Pb 0-06-074522-3   Pb 0-06-082223-6   Pb 0-06-082225-2

#6: Mr. Hynde Is Out of His Mind!

The music teacher, Mr. Hynde, raps, break-dances, and plays bongo drums on the principal's bald head! But does he have what it takes to be a real rock-and-roll star?

#7: Mrs. Cooney Is Loony!

Mrs. Cooney, the school nurse, is everybody's favorite—but is she hiding a secret identity?

#8: Ms. LaGrange Is Strange!

The new lunch lady, Ms. LaGrange, talks funny—and why is she writing secret messages in the mashed potatoes?

#9: Miss Lazar Is Bizarre!

What kind of grown-up *likes* cleaning throw-up? Miss Lazar is the weirdest custodian in the history of the world!

Also look for . . .

#11: Mrs. Kormel Is Not Normal!

Pb 0-06-082229-5

www.dangutman.com